BARE SHADOW

An
Alfaya

Winner of the
Lazarillo Award
for Literary Creation

Translated from Galician by
Jonathan Dunne

GALICIAN
WAVE SMALL
STATIONS
PRESS

To the women with flooded looks
who hid secrets and now talk

The shoes you left behind put on footsteps in the air
which the silence forces me to listen to.

Luis Eduardo Aute, 'Stupid Circular Mania'

1

It was no longer a time of hunger. Earlier, bread had been spread with pork fat, butter or bacon melted in the warmth of the hearth. Then came olive oil sprinkled with sugar on toasted slices. 'A blessed glory!' according to Amadora.

'A blessed glory, that's right!' she would murmur while stirring the contents of the pot.

Elsa never got to try such palatal delicacies. It repulsed her a little to sink her teeth into the crust and feel the soft part soaked with oily currents sliding down the corners of her mouth. Esperanza, her mother, on the other hand, remembered it as a treat from her childhood. Without a doubt, hunger belonged to other times... Now Elsa sweetened her mouth with chocolate, frequently changed her shoes, not only when they were too tight or the leather was worn, but to match a newly bought blouse, although austerity reigned in that household. To be sure, Elsa ignored the feeling of emptiness in her stomach, of cold in her body from a lack of clothes or heaviness in her eyes because of the absence of images with which to nourish a feeling of sleepiness. To say she had never suffered hunger and cold was to affirm an irrevocable reality. Which was why she shouldn't feel guilty...

'... because nobody is born with guilt in the cradle, only with sorrow, my daughter,' Esperanza used to comfort her.

Meanwhile, sitting at the table in silence, Elsa listened to the conversations among the adults, who often spoke of a past in which hunger seemed to have a life of its own, and it struck her as anachronistic to mention this before the food served daily with handcrafted modesty and with generous culinary abandon on days of celebration.

During these conversations of a monotonous bent, hunger would be joined by the word 'war'. Hunger and war were two words that coincided in the language of her grandparents. Xuliano Contreras pronounced the word 'war' with great emphasis because he had actively taken part on the Republican side, and hunger had been relegated to an unimportant second level for the defenders of the cause.

'There was no time back then to think about rumblings in the stomach, only about the crooks who were set on stealing our ideas,' he exclaimed with exaltation, sending a mouthful of red wine down his throat, conjuring up anecdotes in which ideals played a pre-eminent role.

In Amadora's mouth, on the other hand, the word 'hunger' appeared like an exhalation and, as she pronounced it, her eyes flicked towards the steaming dish of newly cooked chickpeas, she dipped her spoon in the potage and gobbled up the broth with predatory voraciousness. In her grandmother's eyes, Elsa discerned a hint of greed where sparks of pain glistened. The hunger of another age had been so devastating that the word 'war' was often joined by another – 'disease' – often accompanied by a cruel adjective: 'incurable'. Amadora would cry, as if reciting a litany:

'War is an accursed female that marries death. She brings along misfortunes and makes scoundrels of people. Few can say they haven't been carried along by her tyranny and committed acts they later regretted… It takes a lot to lift your head when the memories weigh so much… But I always defended the lives of my people before everything else.'

Included among the 'people' she referred to were her children, Fernando and Florinda, as well as a family saga whose members had been extinguished one by one as a result of the aforementioned war, natural diseases, old age and sadness… At that time, Sagrario, her sister, had managed despite the circumstances to survive the lack of encouragement.

2

Elsa grew in an embittered atmosphere of painful evocations of the past. For years, her parents did not add or remove a single comma from the remarks of her grandparents Amadora and Xuliano, who had become the transmitters of an age of conquerors and conquered. That dark world impressed her so much that a seed of anxiety sprouted inside her and, every time she bit into a piece of bread, she felt as if she was betraying her ancestors' memory, the misery of people who lacked the basic means of survival, and she even questioned to what extent she had the right to plan for the future when there were those who lacked a present. Her mind was an oily pool on which floated contradictory sentiments.

'You can take everything away from a girl, except for hope,' Esperanza murmured to herself, disapproving of her mother-in-law's attitude.

Elsa, focusing on the sparks coming out of the stove, wondered why nobody had ever spoken to her clearly about hardly anything at all, certainly not Sagrario. In fact, she wasn't even aware what Grandma Amadora's sister represented in the family circle until she passed away. Seeing that sickly body inside the modest coffin, without the slippery expression that, as far as she could remember, had accompanied her in life and had only left her at the moment of her death, impressed Elsa. She noticed a breathlessness in her throat when she understood that, once Sagrario was buried, no relative would wish to alleviate her burning desire to find out about the deceased woman's guilt. Because if there was one thing she was certain about, it was that a great sense of guilt hung over Sagrario's coffin, at least in the eyes of her grandparents.

Elsa at once became convinced that the dead woman's delicate image was the fruit of earlier hunger, but what she couldn't understand perhaps was why she and her family enjoyed relative well-being, while Sagrario wandered about the house like a ghost, entered the kitchen when everybody had finished their breakfast, lunch or supper, and sat down in the corner, waiting for Amadora to serve her leftovers in a bowl, as if she was a dog. She would remain silent, then get up and shut herself in her room, dragging her feet, avoiding people's eyes in the corridor, trying not to bump into anybody, especially Grandpa Xuliano.

Elsa's natural curiosity forced her to conceal herself and spy on her secretly. More than once their eyes met, which sent a shiver down her spine, although they never went so far as to exchange words, despite her suspicion that Sagrario and Aunt Florinda were hiding a secret. The furtive looks both women gave each other caused Elsa's fervent imagination to travel along unexplored paths.

In Elsa's mind, Sagrario symbolized all the secrets that her grandparents' mouths kept quiet, especially when her walking was silent, not just because of the advance of her feeble body and her moderate pace – her geisha's shuffling gait – but because she walked barefoot. Those naked feet witnessed to the most terrible poverty in the eyes of a girl who couldn't understand why, when the war had finished so many years earlier, her grandmother's sister lived in isolation from the rest of the family, on the margins of their lives. In front of the coffin, her doubts increased. For the first time, Elsa received an image that astonished her: Sagrario's feet were shod in a pair of pretty high heels with a green velvet bow on their uppers, shining so much they hurt the eyes. Elsa wondered what a dead woman needed shoes for if she had walked barefoot all her life. She glanced around at the assembled company – from her grandparents to her parents, passing through her aunt Florinda – but only ever encountered an evasive disposition.

3

Elsa thought a flicker of the eyes, a gesture or significant attitude on the part of her grandparents was enough for her mother to give way before their tacit orders. And yet her father was different. Fernando Contreras did not willingly succumb to impositions. He was an educated man who by dint of circumstances had been forced to support his family with a job that wasn't on his level. According to Amadora and Xuliano, he had married Esperanza to rescue her from hunger. With a posture that was a little overweening, they claimed they had managed to overcome the miseries of war without needing to sell themselves for a bowl of lentils, while the people in their daughter-in-law's house had lived like lice – at the expense of others – betraying the only thing that should never be betrayed: their ideals.

With the passing of the years, Esperanza took it upon herself to explain to Elsa that her grandparents' hatred for her family derived from a time when her family had fought on the side of the Nationalists, some out of conviction, others to banish hunger and fear. Her father had been among the first, and she wasn't exactly proud of this fact, but nor was she going to disown him… The fact that Fernando had dared to woo and then marry her had been a challenge to the principles of Xuliano Contreras, who, following this confrontation with his son, did not speak to him for years, until she, baby Elsa, his first and only grandchild, was born and he decided, on Amadora's advice and for the good of the child, to let bygones be bygones.

'Reds to the core, convinced Republicans, your grandparents' lot,' Esperanza had said to Elsa one time, on their way to the cemetery with Fernando, a walk they often undertook with the excuse of changing their dead ancestors' flowers.

'They are choking on their resentment,' added Fernando, 'and with the passing of the years their blood has turned to bile. They martyred your mother as if she was to blame for the errors committed by her family and truth, that ambiguous thing, was only with them. There are always two sides in war, and both suffer because they are right… But in this small territory of guilt and guilty, they tore into Sagrario, who was perhaps the least guilty of them all.'

'Or not – who knows!' exclaimed Esperanza, leaving the doubt hanging in the air.

Fernando Contreras had a fishbone of sorrow stuck in his throat because of the contemptuous way his aunt Sagrario had been treated. He remembered her from his childhood as a woman of delicate health and weak will who had taken it upon herself to raise his sister, Florinda, and him at a time when Amadora was seeing to the family's needs by means of the black market, a mysterious, sonorous word that filled his childhood with fantasies. It took Sagrario's death for him to give voice to his annoyance and dare to challenge his mother.

'Aren't you going to forgive her even now she's dead? Have a little compassion and don't send her to the other world with nothing on her feet. The poor woman paid enough while she was alive for a crime she committed in her youth.'

'She never took pity, not even on the dead!' declared Xuliano in a fit of pique.

Amadora was disturbed by her husband's coldness – and her own – and for a moment, in spite of everything, her heart softened like a wet sponge releasing the flow of water contained in its porous consistency. That was how Sagrario's feet ended up being cushioned by the very shoes that had once led to her condemnation.

Elsa couldn't forget Fernando's remark while they were winding a sheet around Sagrario, or Xuliano's reply, or Amadora's distorted features, and she clung to them as to a floating piece of wood in her search for easy answers, although she suspected they would be hard to come by.

4

Elsa was no longer prepared to put up with evasive answers, having seen how Fernando Contreras's words had the desired effect on Amadora so that Sagrario could walk in the world of the dead with shoes on her feet, but of all the people around her she suspected only her parents perhaps would dare to speak, since for her grandparents Sagrario represented a sacrilege to the memory of the fallen and for her Florinda was a stranger who came visiting once in a while.

Amadora, after the burial of her sister, on her return to the house, sat down in the kitchen, slowly and carefully removed the black scarf that had covered her grey hair tied back in a ponytail and, while folding it, making sure the corners met and formed perfect squares that got smaller and smaller until the cloth had been reduced to the size of a handkerchief, she sighed. The final sigh coincided with the last fold. Elsa followed the movement of her hands with hypnotized eyes. Her grandmother's exhalation disturbed her sense of fascination, and quite spontaneously a question of hers broke the silence being mutilated by the bubbling of the stew that had started boiling on the stove.

'Will you miss her, Grandma?'

Amadora seemed to wake up from a hallucination. Her lips trembled, but she had no time to answer. Xuliano Contreras came bursting into the sweltering room and arrogantly responded for her:

'"Once the shame is dead, the wound heals."'

'Meaning...'

'Meaning it would be better not to rummage in the wound in case it ends up bursting and getting worse,' he declared.

There were no more remarks, except for those of Esperanza. 'Words are seams,' she murmured.

Elsa's mother liked coming out with the odd phrase while tacking up the bottom of a skirt, holding a button in place or darning some socks. For years now, these had been her tasks. Fernando's had been to head off at sunrise to work in Bieito Nogueira's wood factory.

Esperanza was another shadow in the house, just like Florinda until she got married and Sagrario before she died. Each in their own way lived under the pressure exerted on them by Amadora's inquisitive gaze and Xuliano's imposing presence, consumed by guilt.

Esperanza's guilt was to have been born under a roof of Fascist thinking; she would redeem her pain by stitching up her mouth and not emitting any word louder than the previous one in front of her in-laws. Florinda's guilt was to have been forced to marry a man she didn't love; her affliction, to have turned into a dry female for life. Sagrario's guilt was to have put on the wrong shoes at the wrong time; her sorrow, to wander like a barefoot shadow about the house.

No one witnessed the sense of anguish that settled in Esperanza's heart when she crossed the threshold of that building. No complaint ever left her mouth, although her in-laws took every opportunity to remind her of her origins. She succeeded in silently enduring that lynching that was carried out behind Fernando's back to avoid further warfare in the family, because of the great love she felt for her husband and to save Elsa any unpleasantries. Nor did anyone notice the stomach ache that burst Florinda's insides when she lost her only love. The obligation to marry a man who repelled her etched a bitter expression on her face when she realized with her aunt Sagrario's death her own decline had just begun. Meanwhile, everyone had taken part in Sagrario's suffering – nobody had openly taken pity on her. And yet, when she retired to her room that last night, only Elsa noticed the enigmatic smile bordering her lips, unaware this was a sign of her definitive farewell.

5

In little more than a month after Sagrario's death, Elsa turned sixteen, at the start of the eighties. Fernando Contreras thought the time had come to share with his daughter the secret that tormented her adolescent nights. He took her by the shoulders, and they directed their footsteps towards the path that led to the cemetery. They kept up a normal walking pace. Behind them, several pairs of eyes and the same number of thoughts met in the air while watching them leave from different windows in the house.

Esperanza tried to thread a needle, but couldn't get the strand through the hole. Xuliano, who'd grown old in recent months, rolled a cigarette and muttered oaths. Amadora let the flow of water wash away the lettuce's impurities. Meanwhile the three of them handed Fernando the power of revealing the family's greatest secret to Elsa, which wasn't his own marriage to a Fascist's daughter, nor the business about Florinda, but Sagrario's guilt... He assumed the role and thought it best done in front of her gravestone by talking slowly:

'She was condemned by the rage of all those years of misery, Elsa, not by events. Your grandparents were cruel because other people took it out on their family and they unleashed their anger on a defenceless being that shared their blood. Sometimes human beings respond like that, without thinking, the animal they carry inside pulls at them and... In short, one shouldn't judge them too harshly. My parents' response was the result of pain...'

'And hatred and resentment?' inquired Elsa.

'No. Pain, I think. Hatred and resentment turn people into stakes, pain turns them into erupting volcanoes. Your grandparents allowed their lava to overflow and after that they couldn't hold it back.'

On the morning when the windows of the Contreras Soler family misted up with the breath of an expectant Amadora, Esperanza and Xuliano, as they watched Fernando and Elsa leave for the cemetery, the three of them hoped in the bottom of their hearts that with this gesture of consent, from now onwards, they would cease to avoid each other's gaze and start to forgive each other for past affronts. By their actions or omissions, all of them had contributed to keeping Sagrario's punishment alive, and that was a burden they would have to assume. They remained inactive while father and daughter were out, and only when they saw them reappear on the track did they take up their tasks with a sense of relief in their chests, not knowing what awaited them.

Esperanza succeeded in threading the needle. Xuliano rolled his cigarette and inhaled a large mouthful of smoke that invaded his lungs, only to let it out and release part of his own pride. Amadora let the water wash away the lettuce's impurities and also the remains of the anger that still nestled deep inside her. But none of them could have suspected that the Elsa coming back along the track was not the same as the one who had set out. For that reason, Fernando's words took them aback:

'She wants *you* to do the talking, not me.'

His eyes fixed on Amadora and Xuliano's tense bodies.

'What did Sagrario do that makes you so ashamed and hurts you so much?' spat their defiant granddaughter.

Although Xuliano wanted to take to his heels, Esperanza held him back with her voice, for the first time in all those years of silence succumbing to her wish to express an opinion.

'Elsa's not a child anymore and I don't want to live in this house for another day unless the truth comes out. Enough of mysteries! I hope Fernando can understand and agree with me...'

The aforesaid simply nodded, making it clear he was on Esperanza's side.

6

Amadora served herself a bowl of steaming broth, which she sipped slowly, and ventured to speak. Neither the hoarse engine of the car driven by Bieito Nogueira, Florinda's husband, nor her daughter's subsequent entrance into the house, interrupted her:

'Sagrario was just a girl when this happened... All we had back then were hunger and sorrows... Perhaps the war's to blame... She was just a girl who performed the role of a woman in my absence...'

Xuliano Contreras remained serious, his eyes fixed on the window that overlooked the cemetery where the remains of his ancestors rested, stroking his ashen beard.

'Why do you make excuses for her?' he exclaimed with contorted features, still keeping his eyes on the misted window.

'In my heart, I forgave her a long time ago, but I preferred to remain quiet so as not to upset you,' murmured Amadora, suppressing a sob.

Xuliano Contreras turned on the axis of his body. He threw the cigarette end on the floor and stamped on it angrily, crushing it with the toe of his shoe. His icy eyes surveyed the assembled company forming a semi-circle around him and finally settled on Elsa, who like Fernando years earlier had dared to defy him.

'You have the Contreras's courage in your blood, and that's good, but you lack respect for your elders, and humility...'

'You're not the one to give lessons on humility,' Esperanza went on the attack in support of her daughter's cause, feeling suddenly emboldened. 'If there's something you're guilty of it's pride, and pride was never a good counsellor in times of war or peace.'

Florinda applauded her sister-in-law's daring with her eyes, but kept quiet. Xuliano Contreras might have been expecting Amadora to throw him a lifeline, but she lowered her head, or Fernando, despite their obvious differences, to consider Esperanza's words hurtful or inappropriate. But his son remained silent in the hope that sincerity might enter the house for the first time.

'All right,' Xuliano accepted the challenge, filling his chest with air, with his words and attitude bearing down on his granddaughter. 'You want to know what Sagrario's sin was? Well, here it is. You can judge for yourself... If after what I'm going to tell you, you think I was cruel to her – I mean, *we* were cruel to her – that's your business... All the same, you lack the necessary perspective to understand certain things...'

'Grandpa, I...' stammered Elsa indecisively.

'Be quiet!' ordered Xuliano and, taking control of the situation, he emptied himself: 'The day of Sagrario's twentieth birthday was bad for all of us, but especially for certain people in the village... After midnight, there were knocks on people's doors... We all knew what that could mean... Some fled, others didn't have the opportunity... From our house, they took my father and my brother... they never came back... They took them all out, threw them into gullies, abandoned them in ditches or gave them the coup de grâce in the cemetery... Bastards, sons of whores!'

Xuliano Contreras banged his fists on the table. In that mournful silence, there exploded an outburst of impotence that sent a shiver down the spines of his listeners. There was a lot of pain and rage contained in those words, which he hid behind the trembling of his jaw. Elsa wanted to stop him, but the volcano's burning lava had overflowed and there was no holding back its journey down the side, as it depicted the horror of an age that formed part of its memory.

7

The cooking pot bubbled in the kitchen to the rhythm of panting breath. Amadora groaned with her hands tied up in her apron; Esperanza bit her lips so hard they bled, saddened by the thought her own family had contributed to the massacre of that night in oblivion; Fernando tensed his jaw, anxious to drive away once and for all the ghosts invading the house; Florinda concealed her secrets; and Elsa trembled like a defenceless blade of grass in the middle of a barren field. She needed to seek shelter in her father's protective arms while her grandfather's eyes cracked like crystals of ice.

'The following day was grey,' continued Xuliano. 'We knew at once they had murdered our relatives and others in cold blood for defending their ideals... what horror, what a slaughter, what an atrocious act...! And in the middle of all that impotence Sagrario appeared... She was radiant... The humility of her dress was in stark contrast to the gleam of her feet, she who always wore a pair of clogs, like all the humble women of the village... That morning, she was wearing some new shoes made of green velvet, the most beautiful shoes her eyes had ever seen... Eyes that shone with happiness – or was it sorrow?... Who can be sure?... When we asked her who had given them to her, she said she had found them in the cemetery, she had taken them from a village girl her own age who had been dressed for a party... she wouldn't need them anymore because she was dead, just like her family... Can you imagine? This gesture horrified us... She had stolen some shoes from an innocent girl who was dead, and along with that her dignity! Can you understand?' cried Xuliano Contreras in a broken voice.

'She just wanted to look pretty for one day,' murmured Florinda, defending her aunt's memory. 'She had just turned twenty, and it seems no one had ever given her a present.'

'A horror and a shame, that's what it was! With her macabre gesture, Sagrario brought shame on us all,' reaffirmed Xuliano, who was having difficulty breathing. 'With this single act, she swept away our sense of pride... You had to be there, to know your own people would never return, to try to understand how some shoes could force you to bow your head for the rest of your life... For that reason, I ordered her to take that blasphemy off her feet, and nobody reproached me for it; they all accepted that the punishment was just; she herself imposed her own penance... Her smile changed, her eyes lost their gleam... She realized any sentence would be light in comparison with that sacrilege... I can still hear her saying:

"'From now until the day of my death I shall wander about the house like a barefoot shadow."'

'And that is what she did,' continued Amadora, who had lost her strength. 'Deep down we all thought the punishment had been too great for a sin committed unwittingly in her youth, but we never did anything to correct it... I hope wherever she may be she can forgive us, because we also were her executioners.'

'That's right, there are many ways of killing... and of dying...' murmured Florinda.

The eyes of Xuliano Contreras, Amadora Soler, Esperanza, Fernando and Florinda gazed at Elsa, waiting for some kind of verdict for that liberating confession. All she said was:

'The truth can hurt.'

But there are scars that never disappear, and the wake Sagrario had left behind her was far too deep to vanish with her death, the seeds of which had begun to put out shoots.

8

The Contreras Soler family wanted a gust of fresh air to enter the house after Sagrario's death, as when one decides to open the windows on early spring mornings after a lengthy winter of closed doors and windows and rooms that reek of dampness. So the first order that came out of Amadora's mouth was the following:

'Florinda, daughter, go up to the attic and open the skylight. It's time a little sun entered that nest of woodworm and cobwebs.'

She then aimed a diligent look at her daughter-in-law and added:

'Esperanza, get a move on and open the curtains and the shutters in the rooms, leave the doors wide open so the sun's rays can reach the landing.'

After that, she gestured with her head in the direction of the basement by way of emphasizing a new command, this time aimed at Xuliano:

'Go down to the cellar with care and leave the door ajar so the air can circulate. I think that stench of nostalgia must come from some rotting wineskin. Check the barrels are OK, I don't want us having vinegar instead of wine.'

Fernando patiently awaited his mother's orders, which normally sounded bitter, but today were full of song.

'You, son, go to the stables and let the animals out, poor things, they haven't seen the light of the sun for days.'

After the work had been shared out, Elsa thought it unfortunate to have been excluded from the distribution of tasks.

'What shall I do, Grandma?'

Amadora balanced her flesh as if carrying a ship's set of sails and took several steps forwards until she was close to her granddaughter.

'Go and air that head of yours, creature, you need it.'

Elsa's head, however, was working like a Ferris wheel that doesn't stop turning on its axis. She disliked the idea that Sagrario's death had been a liberation for her grandparents and not a cause of sorrow, as normally happens when you lose a loved one.

'Who is going to air Sagrario's room?' she spat out.

Elsa left the question hanging in the air, provoking different reactions among those present: she read surprise in the faces of Fernando and Esperanza, unease in Amadora, anxiety in Florinda and fury in Grandpa Xuliano, who as he was about to tread on the first step of the stairs that led to the cellar felt his granddaughter's voice sticking in his back like a dagger. He turned around with contorted features, roaring like a wild bull. His face resembled a lit firework.

'Repeat that question!' he boomed.

'Who is going to air Sagrario's room?' replied Elsa defiantly.

'No one is going to air Sagrario's room,' declared Xuliano gravely. 'As long as I'm alive, it will remain shut.' His voice sounded like an order.

Amadora dared to suggest:

'Perhaps Elsa's right, Xuliano. Ever since that business, it hasn't been aired. Sagrario kept the shutters closed and didn't let a trickle of light invade her intimacy.'

'Better that way. There's nothing for us in among her belongings.'

'Are you afraid her ghost is still dancing about the house like a barefoot shadow?' said Elsa ironically.

Fernando and Esperanza gave her a reproachful look.

'Elsa, that's enough!' commanded her father, who wasn't used to raising his voice.

In the end, it was Florinda who spoke, rejecting the head of the household's mandate and surprising everybody with her words. Elsa saw in her eyes a gleam that reminded her of the one that used to paralyze her when she was secretly watching Sagrario, and she again felt a shiver.

'I will air my aunt's room. I'm not afraid of ghosts. Are you?'

9

Amadora thought to herself it hadn't been time for Sagrario to die – she herself was ten years older, and no bodily illness had come to disturb her peace. And yet she got to the conclusion it was ailments of the soul that had relieved her sister of a cruel existence by offering her a premature end. Without Sagrario, her martyrdom would come to an end, she reflected after burying her, feeling happy for the first time, not wanting to show it openly, but with a stab of anxiety rooting around inside, since she suspected Elsa would carry on fiddling with the wounds until they were raw flesh and all the bile came pouring out, as if she wanted to avenge her memory. She hadn't been expecting Florinda, who always obeyed her father's will, to step forwards like that. Suddenly she noticed her daughter existed, had her own presence, body and voice, and, most appallingly of all, had inherited the same glint in her eyes that had glowed in Sagrario's pupils.

The words pronounced by Florinda in the middle of the kitchen cut the air, which had yet to enter the house, although everybody noticed a waft of hot steam that made it difficult for them to breathe.

'I'm not afraid of ghosts. Are you?'

'Open that window, Esperanza,' asked Amadora breathlessly, turning down the stove and unbuttoning the top of her blouse.

Her daughter-in-law obeyed, although she suspected Amadora's sweats had little to do with climatic conditions. Curiously, the window in the kitchen was the only one that got opened, because despite Amadora's wish for a little fresh air to enter the rooms, something had broken.

Xuliano went out into the corridor, having first fixed his gaze on Florinda, convinced perhaps his daughter wouldn't be able to hold it. But that wasn't how it was, and he felt so unprotected he was overwhelmed by a wave of panic, a sense of terror that came from years back, there had been plenty of time since then for his face to acquire toasted wrinkles and his hair and curly beard a smattering of ash. Suddenly his back bent double in the midst of nothingness, and he felt his strength ebbing away. It was Fernando who realized his cheeks had lost their colour, his hands were trembling, his body had gone soft like a flexible blade of grass, he was shrinking inside his loose clothing and losing height. With a sudden stride he alerted the others, who were still immersed in the contradictory sentiments that had been sown by Elsa and Florinda. Amadora moaned when she saw her husband in Fernando's arms, all defenceless, a heap of rags.

'What is it, Xuliano?' she asked, swiftly going over to him.

The aforesaid, being held by his son, endeavoured to stand up and murmured:

'Quiet, woman, don't make a fuss, I just need to rest, that's all.'

But Amadora was unwilling to let destiny take hold of the delicate health that had been affecting Xuliano – who was unused to heeding doctors' advice – for several months and she started to bark orders:

'Fernando, take your father to our room. Esperanza, call Dr Aneiros and bring him up to date… As for you,' she said, fixing her gaze on Elsa and Florinda, 'get out of my sight! It was a bad decision when you thought of naming the deceased. I don't want to hear her name mentioned again in this house. Is that clear? Sagrario was a shadow while she lived, but "once the body is dead, so is the picture," understand?'

Florinda and Elsa understood.

10

Some months earlier, Xuliano Contreras had been diagnosed with a heart condition of some seriousness, which he kept to himself and hid even from Amadora, forbidding Dr Aneiros to talk to her about it, with the promise that he would lead a settled life. Meanwhile, recent events had not helped him to keep his word. After the relevant explorations, the doctor came to the conclusion that Xuliano wasn't going to be able to survive on his own, without his wife's assistance, and so he spoke to her behind the patient's back:

'His health is very delicate, Amadora. A heart condition like this has repercussions for anybody, but especially for a man of his age.'

'How can you know this if you haven't carried out any tests?'

'Amadora, eight months ago, when we were away for a week, supposedly because we'd gone hunting, well, we didn't do any such thing... Xuliano underwent an exhaustive examination, and the results were conclusive. He's been taking medicine behind your back. He needs rest and a lack of excitement... Only time will tell...'

Amadora Soler, who still had the courage of another age drawn on her face, experienced such severe pain it was as if someone had ripped out part of her being. The love she felt for that man was animalistic – if she was left without him, she knew her head would flee to wherever he was.

'Has he had any unpleasant experiences these days?' asked the doctor. 'It's as if he's suddenly lost the will to live.'

'Yes, in fact. Something very unpleasant,' she replied angrily. 'He relived some events from the past that set his blood boiling. If only I'd known he was so poorly!'

'It's not your fault, woman. Xuliano is stubborn – there's no contradicting him! In short, now you know what the situation is, make sure he takes his medication every six hours, and I insist – no unpleasant experiences. All the same, should something untoward happen, you know where you can find me.'

Dr Aneiros was almost family. He put his arms around Amadora's plump body and kissed her on the cheek. She sat down on a stool in the kitchen and wiped away the stream of tears with her apron while watching through the window as the doctor got in his car and disappeared into the distance. She felt empty and alone, unable to tell anyone the great secret that seethed inside her chest. She had always stayed firm in her decision to keep quiet, as if she knew nothing of Xuliano's past liaisons, but she had promised herself that one day, when the children were sufficiently grown up, she would pluck up the courage to reproach him to his face, despite the blind love she felt for him, or else precisely because of that love that had taken root inside her and she had never been able to pluck out. She had never found the right moment to speak to him and was always putting off the time to regain her woman's dignity…

Elsa's birth had given her the perfect excuse to remain silent. She thought it would be cruel for her granddaughter to grow up with a deformed image of her grandfather. And besides, what would she gain by revealing certain details of the past to Fernando and Florinda? She would only sow more pain. In that house, there would never be peace, and all she wanted was peace, even if it was invented and false.

She had finally decided to wait and have a private conversation with Xuliano when the two of them were alone, he smoking a cigarette, as always. She imagined him looking out of the kitchen window, his gaze fixed on the cemetery, while she peeled potatoes, shelled peas or sliced chorizo… But suddenly she realized she wouldn't get another opportunity, because Dr Aneiros's warnings had put her in the difficult predicament of having to choose between regaining her own dignity and potentially becoming his murderer, if she added to his suffering, now that Xuliano was convalescent.

11

As soon as Elsa discerned Florinda's interest in opening Sagrario's room and Xuliano's clear desire that it should remain closed, a mechanism was activated inside her that kept her permanently on tenterhooks, and all her clever daring was aimed at finding out a way to get hold of the key that opened the door, although since Sagrario's death nobody seemed to know where it was. She had a premonition that this summer could yield rich results in her investigations and she decided to act. First of all, she did it openly and went to talk to Esperanza:

'Mother, where is the key for Sagrario's room?'

'I couldn't tell you. I suppose your grandmother has it. What do you need it for?'

'To air the room. Wasn't that what we had agreed?'

'Florinda said she would do it.'

'But Florinda hasn't been back since Grandpa was taken ill.'

'She'll be here any day now. You know Bieito doesn't like her leaving the house very much. She sometimes does it behind his back, when he's at the factory.'

'Why did she marry him?'

'Old alliances.'

'You never give me a straight answer!'

'If you want, ask her yourself. I don't like airing other people's lives.'

'I have a right to know my family's history.'

'What right is that, you brazen hussy? Each person's private life is sacred.'

'Why are you getting angry?'

'I hate you meddling with things from the past. Why don't you act like other girls and worry about things that are suitable for your age?'

'Like what, for example?'

'I don't know! Isn't there some boy who's fallen desperately in love with you?'

'No, Mother, and don't go changing the subject!'

'All right then. I'll spell it out for you. If Grandpa Xuliano realizes you're asking for the key to Sagrario's room, he'll get upset and, according to Dr Aneiros, that could cost him his life. Doesn't your grandfather's health concern you?'

'Of course it does! It's just I don't understand this insistence of his on locking up anything that has to do with Sagrario.'

'You're very young, Elsa. He told you all about it. Sagrario is a blot on his memory. Now he just wants to rest peacefully without having to relive all those moments. Is that so difficult to accept?'

Esperanza talked while sewing a line of thread on the cloth, and Elsa knew her mother would never diverge from that line on the cloth to give her the explanations that would placate her anxiety. Perhaps deep down she was ashamed of her own past and didn't want to rummage through it and have to justify her parents' actions. Elsa would never know, because Esperanza had protected herself over the years with a suit of iron armour so that no one would reach the environs of her heart.

Elsa tried again with Fernando. Her father was normally more malleable, and she almost always managed to bring him over to her territory, but on this occasion she bumped into another brick wall.

'I prefer to respect my father's will. I don't know anything about the key, and nor do I want to.'

'One respects the will of the dead. The living are simply obeyed. Why do you all obey Grandpa?'

'Don't say that about me, Elsa. You know full well I went against him in marrying your mother, which led to years of silence.'

'So why are you obeying him now?'

'I repeat: I'm not obeying him. He is a sick man who can't defend himself. I am respecting his wishes.'

'But he doesn't even have to know. He's been shut up in his room for days. Who's going to tell him?'

'Stories have a habit of sprouting wings, Elsa. Hadn't you realized that, daughter!'

Elsa thought it would take Xuliano's death for that mysterious door that served as a bridge towards Sagrario's secrets to open, and she shivered as she weighed up the possibility of wanting her grandfather to die just so she could sate her own curiosity.

12

There are those who believe that erecting a house with a view of the cemetery is a bad omen; there are those who say the exact opposite. Like his parents and ancestors before him, nobody had asked Xuliano Contreras any such thing, because the house had passed from one generation to the next by means of inheritance. Perhaps the odd person had felt a little uncomfortable about its location, but the fact is they all lived in it – except for the dead, of course, but that wasn't their choice. It might even be affirmed that Xuliano felt a sense of ease when he looked out of the window and descried the niches in the distance. He used to reflect on how his loved ones rested inside them and, sooner or later, he also would take up residence in one of those flowery chalets lined up one on top of the other.

It had never even occurred to Xuliano that Sagrario would die before him, perhaps because she was a woman and was younger. Needless to say, knowing she was buried in the cemetery and considering the possibility that his remains might one day be joined with hers caused him deep anxiety, so that he nosedived into the only hole he wanted to flee, to which it seemed he was now condemned.

'I'm cold,' he muttered with his face wrapped in numerous layers. 'Bring me some blankets, Amadora.'

'That cold you feel won't go away with blankets, Xuliano,' she sobbed.

'Bring me some blankets, dammit!' shouted the sick man, scarcely able to breathe.

Amadora stood up and opened the doors of the wardrobe. On tiptoe, she grabbed another blanket, which she tenderly laid out on top of the others. She sometimes thought her husband would suffocate under all that weight, but he carried on deliriously asking for more.

'Is it better like that?'

'It is… why are you crying?'

'Oh, nothing.'

'Then bring me another blanket.'

In his moments of lucidity, which became rarer as time went by and sometimes didn't even last a day, Amadora wondered whether now would be a good opportunity to talk to Xuliano. She suspected he might be suffering because of the shame of his secret, and it drove her mad knowing he didn't realize she'd always known, even when she'd consented to Sagrario's punishment. But just as she was about to express herself she suddenly noticed an obstacle in her throat, as if a breadcrumb or a fishbone had got stuck there, preventing the air from passing. She only felt like crying, and her apparent courage collapsed in the rocking chair in an attempt to clear her mind of thoughts and find rest in sleep.

One of those afternoons when she had finally managed to shut her eyes, she was alerted by the warmth of someone's breath and the drone of a blowfly in her ear. She opened her eyes and came face to face with her granddaughter.

'Grandma, Grandma…!'

'What on earth…?' she woke up in alarm.

'Grandma, I'm looking for the key,' whispered Elsa urgently.

'What key are you talking about?' she asked, stretching herself.

'The key to Sagrario's room,' replied Elsa, raising her voice.

Amadora leapt from her chair.

'Be quiet, your grandfather sleeps very lightly.'

'Have you got it?'

'What do you want it for?'

The two of them kept whispering – not so much because they didn't want to wake Xuliano as because they suspected he wasn't really asleep.

'It's just I was thinking of changing my room.'

Amadora felt the room spinning like a Ferris wheel and went all dizzy.

'Have you gone mad? What kind of nonsense is that?'

'It's not nonsense. I'm sixteen and need a bigger room. I want to see if I like Sagrario's. Have you got the key?'

A voice from the door, however, replied instead of Amadora: 'No, I have.'

Florinda, who had come in without knocking and had been listening in silence, held up a key in her hand. Her dark presence took them aback and made both grandmother and granddaughter fix their gaze on the wooden woman's silhouette, which was framed by the doorway.

13

Ever since Florinda had married Bieito Nogueira, a man in a good financial position who was twice her age, she had exhibited a bitter appearance. She dressed soberly, and the only visits she paid were to her family, outings that always coincided with the arrival of Avelino, the postman, who for years now had been bringing a registered letter in his sack from Argentina, sent by her childhood friend Isolinita Cruz.

Bieito had never got involved in this correspondence, since he imagined the missives would have to do with affairs that were of scant interest. He concluded that since Florinda led a monastic life and dealt with the household expertly, he could permit her this little whim. Besides, he was convinced that this flow of letters would help her to forget Rafael Xunqueira.

Bieito Nogueira had made his fortune in a way that wasn't entirely clear. He was the owner of the wood factory where most of the men in the village worked, and a moneylender on the side. He possessed lands and a good estate. And yet he had an uncultivated appearance and a reputation for being tight-fisted. Florinda lacked nothing material, but Bieito controlled the capital down to the last cent and gave her just what she needed. He certainly never noticed the trembling of her lips, the gleam in her eyes, the beats that almost burst the poor woman's chest and the shortness of breath that overwhelmed her every time a letter came from Argentina, drawing a splendid rainbow across her face.

Florinda was panting when she took the envelope, signed the receipt and ran to lock it in the chest of drawers in the master bedroom. Once she was sure she was alone, without

Bieito's presence interrupting her palpitations, she would return to the room, nervously insert the key and extract that paper treasure, savouring the moment when she would tear open the envelope and sniff the folded sheet it contained, caressing its texture with the tips of her fingers, relishing the rhythm, the harmony of tenderly written words, kissing the individual letters and giving free rein to the tears that sprang up in her eyes like seeds in a fertile field. Perhaps if Bieito had had his wits about him, he might have suspected something, but since he was more worried about domestic economy than the field of emotions, he interpreted Florinda's floods as the joy of a child who is given a sweet only very rarely.

One day, however, the postman came to their house when Florinda had already gone out, and he was met by Bieito, who didn't like the surprise and distrust displayed by Avelino when he saw him. For the first time, Bieito wondered about the innocence of those letters and wanted to confirm his reservations. When Florinda turned up with a heavy bag of shopping, she spotted something dark in her husband's expression that occupied his mind. Bieito had left the envelope on top of the living-room table. She fixed it with her gaze and felt a shiver run down her spine. She prayed it hadn't been opened. Her husband remarked casually:

'You have a letter from Isolinita.'

She took a rapid step forwards and stretched out her hand like a cat's paw. This gesture gave her away. Bieito was abruptly confronted by the evidence. Despite his coarseness, he also had learned to adopt a façade and he added:

'It's about time you shared something of Isolinita's news, how are things in Argentina?'

Florinda stayed upright when she heard this question and managed to keep her composure as she replied:

'Very well. Her fourth child is on the way.'

'Please give her my congratulations.'

After that, no more letters from Argentina ever made their way to Bieito Nogueira's residence.

14

Amadora forced Elsa and Florinda to leave the room in which Xuliano Contreras was resting.

'I don't want a hullabaloo. What do you think this is – some kind of party?'

She pushed them along the corridor and went back in. She closed the door behind her and sat in the rocking chair next to the bed, sunk in the shadows of the room. She soon discerned the voices of her granddaughter and daughter, who were whispering on the other side of the wooden leaf.

'Curiosity is a bad counsellor, Elsa.'

'I don't think so… Why do you have the key to Sagrario's room if you don't live here?'

'Because I'm the only one who has the right. Everybody else turned their back on her.'

'You too.'

'What do you know? I wanted to take Sagrario to live with me, but Bieito wouldn't have it.'

Xuliano stirred beneath the sheets. The whispers penetrated the cracks in the door and sounded like the drones of blowflies invading his solitary territory.

'Who's that whispering, Amadora?'

'Florinda. She's in the corridor, giving Elsa an errand.'

'Tell them to be quiet.'

Amadora made as if to get up to banish the noise, but suddenly the voices fell silent. Florinda and Elsa had gone out into the yard. Esperanza stared at them through the kitchen window while checking on the stove. Ever since Xuliano had been taken ill and Amadora had gone to sit with him, she had assumed her mother-in-law's role and taken responsibility for domestic affairs. She liked running the household and felt in a better mood. When Fernando came back from the factory, he noticed a happy expression on her face, which was in stark contrast to the ashen look on Amadora's face whenever she entered or left the sick man's room, which upset him somehow.

Days earlier, having discovered Xuliano's condition, Amadora had handed the keys of the house to Esperanza, affording her in this way a confidence she had never shown her during years of cohabitation. She only kept one, which she then privately delivered to Florinda.

'Keep it. You'll know what to do with it. I don't mind if you chuck it in the bottom of a well and never handle it again,' she had said to her daughter, with coldness in her eyes.

Florinda breathed a sigh of relief when she got hold of the key to what had been Sagrario's prison and she was grateful to her mother for this gesture of confidence. Neither of them had been expecting Elsa, for whom the trunk of the many mysteries that danced around the house had now been opened, to maintain her interest in the deceased woman's room.

'I know you used to visit Sagrario on the quiet,' she spat at Florinda.

'So what? Didn't I tell you my wish was to have her come and live with us?'

'Right. And wasn't there something else between you?'

'What do you mean?'

'I don't know, it's for you to tell me!'

Florinda's years of adolescence were far behind her and she failed to interpret her niece's sense of irony. If with her words she was insinuating some kind of morbid relationship between her and Sagrario, then perhaps, now that she was dead, it would do her good to carry on speculating in that direction, since there was no way of proving it and, when it came down to it, Elsa was just a young girl with an ardent imagination.

'Now she's not here,' continued the girl, 'don't you think I'd better have the key?'

'No, I don't.'

Florinda's response was emphatic. She displayed not the slightest hint of doubt in her eyes. She had the disputed key in her hand and made as if to put it in her pocket, but at that precise moment Elsa was quicker and snatched it from her, running into the house. Florinda's face fell, and she started shouting after her. Esperanza watched the scene unfold from the kitchen and made to go out into the yard. In the corridor, she bumped into Elsa, who was fleeing with a naughty expression along the corridor towards the upper floor. With a sense of powerlessness, Florinda covered her face with her hands and burst into tears, just as she heard Bieito tooting the horn.

15

Bieito Nogueira's estate and Xuliano Contreras's property were separated by just a few plots of land, several cart tracks that had been conditioned for tractors and private cars, and half a dozen houses dotted about fields of potatoes and maize.

Florinda used to cover the distance between them on foot, especially in the latter part of the afternoon, when the summer temperatures decreased and she could perceive the swish of the grass beating against her legs and the scent of the fruit trees as she passed. She liked to walk in silence, happy with her thoughts, stroking with the tips of her fingers the edges of the letter from Argentina, which she kept in her apron pocket. But out of the blue, coinciding with Bieito's encounter with the postman, her husband had said:

'It's not good for you to walk along those paths on your own.'

'Dr Aneiros told me that stretching your legs is good for the circulation.'

'I don't want your name on people's lips.'

'What do you mean?'

'Just tell me when you want to visit your parents, and I'll take you in the car and come and fetch you afterwards.'

After that, Florinda's walks to the house of her parents had turned into short trips alongside Bieito that lasted barely a few minutes. The missive from Argentina, which she was now obliged to collect directly from the post office behind her husband's back and with the postman's complicity, normally travelled with her, hidden in her apron pocket. Her heart was all entangled. Shortly before Sagrario's demise, Isolinita Cruz's letters had stopped coming, and Florinda, unable to comprehend their absence, would pass in front of the post office, where she knew by a system of signs agreed on beforehand whether she should stop and enter or carry on.

Her visits to her childhood home became less frequent, especially after Sagrario died. There wasn't much to go for, except to recover what was her own... So she leapt with pleasure when she was entrusted with the key. She needed to get into her aunt's room at any cost. But she hadn't counted on her niece's curiosity. 'That girl's a damn nuisance!' she thought when she entered her parents' bedroom and heard Elsa demanding the key from her grandmother, and then she recalled her irony during their conversation in the corridor and the yard. 'I'm going to have to teach her a lesson for sticking her nose in where it's not wanted!' she reflected. Suddenly, however, the girl's gesture, taking advantage of the arrival of Bieito's car at the iron gate and snatching the key from her hands, left her feeling deflated. She didn't have the strength to go running after her. She wasn't a young girl anymore. How could she justify all that commotion in front of Amadora, who was watching over Xuliano as if he was at death's door? Esperanza's look, asking without words what Elsa had done to make her cry, didn't make it easier to talk. To get her sister-in-law to rebuke her daughter and force her to hand over the talisman that protected her secret was not a good method. She would have to pray that if Elsa entered Sagrario's room, she wouldn't rummage about too much. It was foolhardy to think it might occur to her to remove the bedspread, and then the sheets, and notice the frayed seam on the mattress. That was far too convoluted, she decided.

Bieito's insistent tooting of the horn, with the engine running, diverted her attention. She wiped her tears on the sleeve of her jacket and turned around, endeavouring to adopt an ambiguous expression. If he noticed something that alarmed him – as indeed he did – then she could always come up with an excuse.

'Is your father worse?'

'Yes, he's very poorly,' she said in order to say something, without realizing that she wasn't actually lying.

Esperanza, who had taken up position at the kitchen window once more, soon forgot her daughter's mischief, but not Florinda's tears.

16

Elsa noticed her blood was boiling. Why this key had suddenly turned into a talisman, even she didn't know. She couldn't say where her anxious wish to open Sagrario's room and rummage in its corners had come from. She drove away an image that came into her mind. She recalled Sagrario's face the day she died, before she went to bed, and considered the possibility that the deceased woman was pushing her from the beyond to make her act in this compulsive way, she who usually had a calm temperament. The saliva got stuck in her throat, her breathing became irregular, a layer of sweat appeared on her forehead, she felt her body to be light, as if she was a gazelle climbing the stairs in her flight from Florinda, convinced she wouldn't follow her, because Bieito was waiting in the car with the engine running, and he didn't like to be made to wait.

In effect, she wasn't wrong in her deductions. She reached the upper floor, walked across the whole landing, slowing down, and got to the window at the end, from where she could look out into the yard. She saw Florinda getting into the impressive car with its ancient bodywork and line and occupying the seat next to the driver. She heard the brusque sound of the engine as it gathered speed and then saw the car disappearing down the cart tracks. She was still flustered, but she experienced an agreeable sense of freedom. With Florinda gone, Esperanza busy in the kitchen, seeing to the family's needs, Amadora watching over Grandpa Xuliano, neither of whom was likely to abandon the room in which they spent most of the day and night, her grandfather taken up with his illness and her grandmother afraid as soon as she left the room he would give up the fight, with Fernando at the factory and the key in her hand, Elsa said to herself there was nothing to prevent her from opening the door to Sagrario's room and satisfying her curiosity, which had become almost a state of anxiety.

She walked back across the landing, slowly this time, on tiptoe, heading straight for a door that was placed right in front of the staircase and to its left. It frightened her to feel the beating of her heart so clearly through her clothes. Florinda had said she wasn't afraid of ghosts, she had even challenged her family, asking if they were afraid of them, assuming perhaps they believed in apparitions. But Elsa belonged to a generation for whom the existence of creatures from beyond the grave belonged to the narrative of films or novels. Beyond a shadow of a doubt, she could affirm she didn't believe in them. She didn't know what she was going to find behind Sagrario's door, but she certainly wasn't expecting to bump into her erratic soul seeking alms or consolation after the sorrows of this life. So when she put the key in the lock, she had to ask herself, 'Why are you so nervous?' And as she performed the first and second turn, she couldn't come across an answer, but her sense of disquiet only increased, especially when she placed her hand on the doorknob and caused it to turn 180 degrees, noticing how the wooden leaf pulled away from the doorframe, creating a vertical band of darkness, which she then pushed further open. The hinges made not a sound, as if they were well oiled. She was received by absolute darkness, the tick-tock of a clock that, unlike Sagrario's heart, carried on beating at a mechanical rhythm, and a refreshing aroma of laurel.

17

Elsa felt on the wall for the light switch. It wasn't difficult to find. A sudden burst of light swept across the room. She gazed at it and was surprised at how clean it was. She'd imagined coming across a dirty room with chips on the walls and clothes abandoned on the floor. And yet she found a strange order. Then she thought perhaps Amadora had tidied up after Sagrario died. The wake for the deceased had not been in her room, but in the one Florinda occupied when she was single, the transfer of the body, once Dr Aneiros had certified her death, being ascribed to the fact her own room wasn't presentable. Elsa was convinced her grandmother had had a hand in the cleaning. She felt a little disappointed when she took a few steps forwards and noticed the sense of nervousness that had overwhelmed her had abated somewhat. She wasn't sure what she had been expecting to find, but she felt let down. A floral carpet with faded colours, a bed made of fine wood, two matching nightstands, each with a bedside lamp on an embroidered cloth, an alarm clock, the workings of which she had heard as soon as she opened the door, a crucifix above the bedhead, a dressing table with porcelain figures, a wardrobe against the wall, a clothes rail, a curtain of thick material that stopped the smallest ray of light coming in through the window... And on the wooden ceiling, hanging from the beams, pale laurel leaves that still exuded a powerful scent. There was no family portrait, no photo of Sagrario, on any of the furniture.

The more Elsa surveyed the room, the less she understood Xuliano's interest in keeping it closed, Florinda's look of anxiety when she snatched the key, even Esperanza and Fernando's unwillingness to help her get in. The idea of changing room lost its appeal. It wasn't much bigger than her own. She soon decided to leave the room and return the key to Florinda, apologizing for her mad behaviour.

But before abandoning the shadow-infested room once and for all, she was overwhelmed by a wave of curiosity and decided to investigate further. She went over to a nightstand and opened a drawer. She found a pair of shoes. That wasn't the likeliest place to keep shoes, she thought, but there they were, a black, patent-leather pair. She opened another drawer. And came across another pair. She went around the bed and headed for the other nightstand. She found two pairs of shoes: some open, summer ones and some closed, winter ones. With unrest digging in the depths of her stomach, she opened the drawers of the dressing table and the doors of the wardrobe. Except for the space taken up by clothes hanging from the clothes rail, the rest was occupied by a heap of shiny shoes that looked brand new and, knowing Sagrario's story, Elsa understood this could only be the fruit of an obsession. She stretched out her hand and took a shoe at random. She let her fingers run over the leather surface. She shivered when she thought Sagrario might have made that same gesture at another time and she felt naked, as if she was under surveillance. She was just about to put the shoe back in the drawer when she noticed the midsole was slightly loose on one side and what looked like a scrunched-up piece of paper was poking out. She pulled on it gently, afraid it might break. It was a thin sheet of quarto folded in such a way it had been stuck between the insole and outsole of the shoe. Before unfolding it, she was assailed by a suspicion. She took another shoe and had a look. The sole had also been lifted and held another piece of paper inside. Her inspection was unstoppable. An itching in her throat told her now was not the time to abandon that room.

18

Bieito Nogueira respected Florinda's silence. She was a woman of few words and they rarely had much to talk about. He was one of those who think a silent woman is worth double. He had got into the habit of taking and fetching her from her parents' house ever since Isolinita Cruz's letters from Argentina had stopped coming to the house, after he signed for one of them. He suspected the missives might have continued, but he preferred not to dig in the wound, since he lacked a real reason to believe the messages contained something dark that had kept him from seeing for years. He thought sooner or later he would clarify the situation and then he would take the necessary action.

During those visits, he never entered the Contreras's home with Florinda. He had nothing against her family, just some half-finished business from the past. And yet there was no reason for him to behave like a son-in-law who takes an interest in his wife's parents. It didn't bother anybody, not even Xuliano and Amadora, who were grateful for his absence.

Bieito drove at a moderate speed along the cart tracks – if there was something he truly valued, it was his car, and he endeavoured to make sure no tiny scratch detracted from the gleam of the bodywork and no unusual noise caused him alarm about the engine.

On the same afternoon when Elsa deprived Florinda of the key to Sagrario's room, on the return journey, when they were halfway, Bieito Nogueira's car overtook Avelino, the postman, out of uniform, his day's work over, since he lived in those parts. It was some time since the correspondence addressed to Florinda had abruptly and inexplicably ceased, which crumpled her heart and put her on edge, a change of mood she explained to her husband by the logical concern she felt for her father's condition.

Florinda was still trying to get over her niece's behaviour when she thought she discerned in Avelino's expression a sign that indicated some mail was waiting for her. It was just an impression, because Bieito, who had been instructed in customs of yore, didn't like her aiming a look at persons of the opposite sex, since he believed that could be interpreted by the persons in question as a kind of provocation. And yet Florinda's expression changed, she found it difficult to hide the shift in her mood from her husband. From then and for the whole night, her thoughts centred on two obsessive ideas: first, getting back the key; second, finding a way to pay the postman a visit. Her head turned into a cauldron. 'I have to get that key back at any cost. The meaning of my life is hidden in the stuffing of a mattress. I don't think Elsa will rummage about, that would be a lot to expect from her, but who knows?... This niece of mine doesn't stop until she gets what she wants. She didn't stop until she unravelled the mystery of Sagrario's guilt, despite having to confront my father... I also have to speak to Avelino. It may just be my imagination, but I could swear I saw in his face... Perhaps it's just my eagerness to receive news... I don't know, this night is lasting longer than it should. With all this tossing and turning I'll wake Bieito and... I can't imagine how it is he suspected nothing during all these years... But why would he? What harm can there be in two old friends who live far away staying in touch?'

And yet Florinda sensed something had changed in Bieito's attitude and she was afraid of the consequences.

'A wounded Bieito doesn't reason like a normal person,' she mused, 'but explodes like an animal. He is primitive in his reactions when anyone goes against him, which is why he goes through life looking like a bull. It's as if he was waiting for the chance to act... He's capable of killing when it comes to his honour.'

19

Elsa noticed an itching sensation growing in her stomach as she went through Sagrario's shoes and found bits of paper in the midsoles. Suddenly she thought she heard the sound of some footsteps climbing the stairs... She decided to hold back on reading their contents and quickly stuffed a sheet in the pocket of her jacket. Now that she had the key, which she soon resolved not to give back to Florinda, she would come back another time and calmly go through the others. 'Nobody keeps something in a place like that unless they're hiding a secret,' she pondered, suspecting that Sagrario had concealed a great mystery. She still had time to stick her delicate fingers inside another shoe, where she felt the scrape of something hard. She pulled it out carefully. She soon had an old photograph in her hand, which on closer inspection revealed the image of a young, tall and attractive man. It had been cut down the middle, using a pair of scissors, and still showed the shoulder, arm and hand of a woman, on the last of which could be seen a ring. Elsa wondered who the man and woman were, as she listened to the footsteps drawing closer. Perhaps Sagrario had had a boyfriend before she shut herself up in her room? She wondered whether it had been a forbidden love, otherwise if she was the woman, it wouldn't be ripped. Had she had a relationship with a married man? Her enthusiasm was so boundless she didn't realize the footsteps had come to a halt. The turning of the door handle alerted her.

'What are you doing here?'

Esperanza's voice took her by surprise. Elsa still had time to place the photo in the palm of her hand and slam the dressing-table drawer shut.

'I came to air the place,' she explained to her mother, who was standing in the doorway.

'Well, I don't see that you've opened the curtains or the window!' she remarked ironically.

'I was just about to,' she added.

And saying this, with a quick movement, she opened the curtain and the two shutters. The sunset came in through the windows, and a pale light endowed the room with a diluted clarity.

'Leave it, now is not the time,' ordered Esperanza. 'What were you doing rummaging through the drawers?'

'I was just having a look.'

'Did you find what you were looking for?'

Elsa shrugged her shoulders, uncertain how to answer.

'There are lots of shoes,' she said finally.

A smile flickered across Esperanza's lips. She relaxed her inquisitive tone and remarked:

'You can blame your father for that!'

'My father?' exclaimed Elsa, surprised by this revelation.

Esperanza went out on to the landing and peered down the stairs to make sure Amadora had not abandoned her refuge of the last few weeks. She then murmured:

'You know your father has a good heart. He loved Sagrario dearly, she was like a second mother to him, and he couldn't bear to see what a miserable life she was leading, so on her birthday, without your grandparents knowing, he always gave her a pair of shoes.'

Elsa was comforted by this emotional explanation and verified once more that the devotion she felt for her father was not unfounded. And yet another doubt assailed her:

'What did Sagrario want so many shoes for if she never went out and always walked around barefoot?'

'It was just symbolic, daughter, for her to know your father was on her side... Between you and me, I think she liked to put them on and walk about the room – sometimes you could hear the sound of clacking heels on the ceiling of the kitchen. When that happened, I would just turn up the radio.'

From the ground floor came the sound of the hinges of the door of Xuliano and Amadora's room, followed by the slow shuffling of Amadora's slippers along the corridor.

'Out quickly!' commanded Esperanza.

Elsa obeyed. She gently closed the door and winked at her mother. She was about to show her the photo she'd hidden in her hand, but a note of caution made her change her mind. She simply asked:

'Did Sagrario have a boyfriend when she was young?'

Esperanza's expression changed to one of annoyance, and she headed downstairs.

20

Bieito Nogueira, like Florinda, perceived a silent message in the postman Avelino's expression, which he confirmed when he saw the sudden change in his wife's mood and the restless night she spent, tossing and turning in the bed and wandering about the house in the dark, but he pretended to sleep and started coming up with a way to penetrate the tangle of her concealment.

At dawn, after breakfast, he left the house. Earlier, in the kitchen, Florinda, still in her dressing gown, had been washing the dishes in the sink, with her back to Bieito, while he dipped his toast in his coffee. Despite not being a consummate observer, he could see she was still nervous, because every now and then a piece of soapy crockery slipped out of her hands. He drank up his coffee, stood up and gave her a routine peck on the cheek. She used this opportunity to dry her hands on the apron and release the remark that had been clinging to her tongue:

'I think I might go over to see my parents…'

'But you were there only yesterday!' he exclaimed, acting all surprised.

'… it's just my father wasn't well, and…'

'Say no more about it, woman. If that's all it is, you can count on me.'

Florinda realized at once she hadn't done things properly – what she'd really wanted was to get Bieito's permission to go walking to her parents' house that morning, so she could stop off at the post office along the way. Now her hand was forced, she added a little unnaturally:

'If it's a problem, don't worry. I can always go mid-morning. Anyway, I was planning to go to the shop…'

The only shop in that place was two doors down from the post office. Bieito pretended not to notice the detail and made up his mind to play along, since he knew from her behaviour she would fall into the trap.

'Go then. You're right. That will give me time to have a siesta after lunch.'

Florinda was surprised by this sudden acquiescence on his part, since recently Bieito hadn't let her out of his sight, always wanting to know where she was going, but she focused on the happiness of knowing while he was at the factory, she would be able to move about freely, albeit with due discretion, and go to see Avelino and Elsa to reclaim what was hers.

For his part, Bieito left the house with the conviction that he would obtain the key to Florinda's secret that very morning. He sat behind the steering wheel of his car, feeling his wife's uneasy gaze on the back of his neck, but he didn't go to the factory, as had been his original intention. He was the boss and could permit himself the luxury of arriving late. He didn't have to explain his arrivals or departures to anybody. He headed for the town square, which he reached a few minutes later. Everything was close at hand. He encountered several locals, who greeted him with forced cordiality. He was a rich and respectable personage, and most of the men worked in the wood factory that belonged to him. He strode in the direction of the post office, which was located in some ground-floor premises of a few square metres, on the first floor of which Dr Aneiros had his surgery, and was equipped with a counter and a few shelves containing correspondence. The only employee was Avelino, who handled the distribution of items as well, so he usually saw to customers until midday, then closed and with a full sack carried out home deliveries. In the afternoons, he stayed inside, looking after the accounts of Bieito's company under the supervision of a hired clerk. When Avelino saw Bieito come in, he sensed he hadn't come to inquire about the factory accounts. He surreptitiously took hold of a letter and slipped it under the counter. But the gesture did not escape Bieito's notice.

21

As Bieito was heading for the post office, Amadora was coming out of Xuliano's room with the intention of asking Esperanza to prepare some broth, since the sick man insisted the cold wouldn't leave him. She bumped into her daughter-in-law and granddaughter in the corridor. Esperanza was shocked by her weary expression, the black bags under her eyes and the colourless cheeks. Elsa thought her grandmother had aged a multitude of years in a matter of weeks.

'I was looking for you,' she said to Esperanza. 'Be a darling, would you, and heat up some broth for Xuliano? The poor man can't get rid of the sensation of cold.'

'Shall I make something for you?'

'I'm not hungry. I'm going to the toilet.'

'Would you like me to call Dr Aneiros?'

'I'm not sure… I think he's worse, but why bother him…?'

Amadora set off walking, carrying the heavy weight of her body on her slippers, and Esperanza felt sorry for her. All her courage had disappeared – all that was left was a woman who had been overcome by pain. Elsa watched the scene unfold and thought their roles had changed. She had always imagined her grandmother as the strong one in the family, and her mother as the weak. Unwittingly, Xuliano had overseen a shift in power. 'Life is always topsy-turvy,' her father used to say. Fernando preferred to linger in the background, on the margins of everything. He felt disconnected, like Elsa.

Esperanza interrupted her train of thought. She gave her a tug and whispered in her ear:

'Go to Dr Aneiros's surgery and tell him to come as soon as he can... Oh, and give me back the key to Sagrario's room. I think you've had a good look around.'

Elsa was disgusted by her mother's imposition. She was relieved she had been sufficiently bright to keep some of the objects of her spying, which had stopped her getting any sleep for part of the night. Even so, she took the key and handed it over. Esperanza placed it in her pocket and muttered:

'Florinda should have it, you see?'

Elsa nodded and went out into the yard. She passed through the gate with the intention of performing her errand. She started walking along the track that led to the cemetery. It wasn't too hot, despite the fact it was high summer. At a reasonable pace, it wouldn't take her long to reach the town square. Elsa couldn't understand why Grandpa Xuliano refused to install a phone in the house, along with other technological advances. Fernando had said on more than one occasion that the patriarch would have to die before modernity entered their lives. It hurt her again to think she wanted these changes to come about, so she could enjoy some of the advantages that were normal for girls her age.

She was still carrying the impression she had received on learning the contents of Sagrario's shoes and didn't want to prolong the tension caused by the secret in her pocket. She decided to stop and sit on a crag. She looked around. She couldn't see a soul. Just fields of maize, potatoes and fruit trees. She put a hand in her pocket and pulled out the photo. She gazed at it once more. She was familiar with it by now. She had had time to inspect it during the night. The man possessed that ancient charm displayed by heart-throbs in the old films that were sometimes shown at the town's cinema, while the woman's hand with the ring was a kind of mysterious temptation... She turned the photo over and experienced again the emotion of reading the handwritten letters she had discovered beneath the sheets that morning: 'Always yours, X.' She took the letter and unfolded it nervously. She knew the contents almost by heart, the paper wrinkled and rubbed by the passing of her fingers. Suddenly she felt remorse. What was she doing stopping on the way? Her obligation was to go and fetch Dr Aneiros... Her grandfather's life could be in danger... She put the photo and letter away and hurried along, a strange disquiet pricking her insides.

22

Bieito Nogueira approached the postman side-on by asking about the factory accounts and telling him how content the clerk was with his collaboration. He then praised the way he combined his work as postman with that of accountant, especially when it came to carrying out the deliveries as well.

'You're doing very well, Avelino. It's obvious you're a man of many resources.'

The postman nodded and played along, suspecting the motive for his visit was something entirely different.

'Don't believe it, Don Bieito. There isn't much correspondence in a place like this, and the delivery is over before it's begun.'

'You're right. We're only a handful, and who's going to take any interest in us?'

'That's what I mean! Most of the letters are addressed to the wood factory, which after all is what the village lives on.'

'As well as what comes from abroad,' remarked Bieito with a cunning sense of irony. 'There are still lots of countrymen who wish to know about those of us who manage to keep the place alive... Some would like to come back, even if it's only to die.'

Avelino understood what he was driving at, but pretended he didn't.

'One's homeland – it pulls like a magnet.'

Bieito Nogueira, realizing he wasn't going to get where he wanted this way, turned the conversation around:

'Well, Florinda's friend, Isolinita Cruz – you remember her, don't you? the one who left for Argentina some years ago – she used to send a registered letter every month as regular as clockwork, but now...'

'There's lots of water in the middle, Don Bieito, who knows what could have happened on the other side of the sea! Argentina's so far away...'

'I know, Avelino, I know... But there wouldn't happen to be a letter from her that's just arrived?'

'Well...'

'I could swear Florinda said she would be dropping by... and you know, I said, don't worry, woman, I have to talk to Avelino about the company accounts this morning, so I'll ask him about the letter and pick it up for you.'

Avelino's face adopted an expression that was a mixture of incredulity and surprise – if he hadn't told Florinda directly about the letter, how could her husband know about it? He soon realized this conversation was a strategy on Bieito Nogueira's part to get him talking and to make off with his wife's correspondence.

'I couldn't say there's nothing here,' he feigned, pointing to a sack that was brimful with letters, 'but I haven't had a chance to sort through that lot yet. They've been there for three days... Despite all your compliments, I don't seem to manage to get round to everything.'

Bieito lost his patience. He was fed up of playing games and went straight for the postman's jugular.

'Enough tomfoolery, Avelino!' he shouted impatiently. 'Take the letter you hid under the counter and give it to me now!'

'Bu, but...' stuttered the postman, floored by his own lack of caution.

'No buts! Hand it over, or you may find yourself without a means of providing for your family!'

Avelino felt the blood warming his neck and a shortness of breath born of impotence in his throat. He was on the verge of resisting and maintaining the reserve he'd promised Florinda, but Bieito's threat won the day. He knew full well he was capable of carrying it out without the slightest remorse. He put his hand under the counter and pulled out an envelope. He lifted it slowly and placed it on top. Bieito smiled with satisfaction and went so far as to give him a pat on the back.

'That's the way, Avelino! I'll have a word with the clerk and see if we can't give you a raise this month.'

The postman lowered his head in shame, and Bieito took the envelope in his hand. He placed it in his pocket, his chest all puffed up like a robin's, and turning around headed for the exit. Avelino's feeble voice held him back:

'You have to sign for the letter, Don Bieito.'

'Sign? I clean forgot! Florinda can do it some other time.'

23

Elsa's arrival in the town square coincided with Bieito Nogueira's visit to the post office. She noticed his car parked nearby and wondered whether Florinda would be with him. For the last few hours, she'd been thinking about her aunt in a different way...

Dr Aneiros's surgery, located on the first floor of the same building, had a separate entrance that could be reached by a set of stairs, from the landing of which Elsa watched her uncle by marriage leave the ground floor on his own and head towards his vehicle. She made no attempt to greet him because Bieito was somewhat reserved in his relations with the family, and she had no intention of changing this.

Bieito and Florinda's story was another mystery Elsa had set herself the task of unveiling that summer. Without further ado, she entered the doctor's surgery. In the waiting room there was a woman with a child, an elderly man and a young woman. She greeted them, not just out of politeness, but because they were neighbours. She went over to Mariola, Dr Aneiros's wife, who was seated behind the reception desk and who looked after the running of the surgery from picking up the phone to writing out receipts, seeing to visitors' needs and helping the doctor attend the sick when there was nothing to do in reception.

'Hello, Elsa, what brings you here?'

'I've come to tell the doctor my grandfather is worse.'

'Oh dear, is he very bad?' Mariola grew alarmed.

Elsa shrugged her shoulders, uncertain how to reply.

'Well, he's seeing a patient at the moment,' apologized Mariola, 'but I'll give him your message and, as soon as he's finished, he'll come around to your house.'

Elsa thanked her and left the surgery. Mariola was always pleasant to deal with. As she crossed the square, she noticed Bieito's car wasn't there anymore. She started walking quickly back the way she had come. She was about to reach her house when she recalled the contents of the letter in her pocket, which, after she'd read them the night before, had caused her great consternation. In the top right-hand corner, she had read the words 'Buenos Aires', but the ink with the date had been blurred. She had then moved on to the opening. The only words to have collided with her retinas had kept her awake. She murmured to herself, 'Dear Florinda...' She had mentally gone through the rest of the letter without lingering over the contents until she got to the signature: 'Rafael Xu...' The rest of the surname, like the date, had been a smudge. Excited and nervous, Elsa had recalled the short phrase on the back of the photo of the stranger she'd found: 'Always yours, X.' So – she had thought – this 'Xu...' must be the surname of Rafael, the same Rafael Xunqueira who was sometimes talked about by her elders in relation to Florinda. In the midst of all the confusion, she had begun to see the light. Of course! How innocent she had been! This wasn't a photo of some boyfriend of Sagrario's, but of Florinda's! That was why her aunt had been so keen to get into the deceased woman's room! She had wanted to retrieve her correspondence... Perhaps Sagrario had acted as a go-between for years, behind Bieito's back. Everything started to make sense.

Elsa stopped and had another look at the photograph. She noticed, given its obvious antiquity, the man was quite a lot older than Florinda. But it was just an impression, since she couldn't be sure of its date. Then she thought perhaps her aunt liked older men – after all, she'd married Bieito, who was more like a father to her than a husband. Having read the letter, which contained so much love and pain and referred to a past that was now beyond reach, she suspected Bieito had been an obstacle that destiny had placed between Florinda and Rafael.

24

Florinda let Bieito drive off in the direction of the wood factory without suspecting he was going to take a detour to the post office when he was halfway. Had she known this, she would not have been so content, thinking she had the whole morning in front of her to fulfil her objective. She quickly tidied the kitchen, prepared lunch in case her errands took longer than expected, dressed discreetly, without adornments or make-up, as was her custom, bolted doors and windows and set out to confirm once and for all whether her premonitions were certain and a letter from Rafael was waiting for her. She ordered her legs to take her to the town square and, flitting from one thought to another, she considered it was perhaps more urgent to visit her family home and try to persuade her niece to give her back the key to Sagrario's room, because if Elsa decided to go off somewhere early, then her whole plan would collapse; after all, the letter from Argentina was safely in Avelino's keeping.

She hadn't wandered down these paths for quite some time and she was grateful for the walk. The temperature was pleasant, a light breeze caressed her face. She almost bumped into Elsa, but didn't realize this until Esperanza, who had been astonished to see her entering the gate, came out to meet her and asked in surprise:

'What are you doing here so early?'

'I've come to see Daddy... I'm busy this afternoon.'

'Come in then... Poor man, he's not long for this world... Elsa's just gone to fetch Dr Aneiros, did you not meet her on the way?'

Esperanza's words were like a stab in the back for Florinda.

'You mean she's not here?'

'Why, no! Did you want to talk to her?'

Florinda felt cold in the doorway and didn't reply. She took a few steps forward and entered the kitchen, where a warm broth was bubbling away. Esperanza went after her.

'Would you like a bowl?' she offered.

'I wouldn't mind. I'm a little out of sorts. The lack of habit, now Bieito always brings me in the car.'

'Didn't he mind you coming out today…?'

'Actually, he didn't. I was surprised, but thought he realized I wanted to see Daddy, since he's so poorly.'

'Yes, of course.'

Florinda sat on a stool, and Esperanza served her a bowl of steaming broth.

'You'd better blow on it, it's hot!' she warned. She then sat down next to her, and Florinda noticed she wanted to say something, but didn't dare.

'Florinda,' began Esperanza eventually, lowering her voice so Amadora wouldn't hear. 'You don't have to pretend with me. Fernando and I have known for years and we respect your secret. Sagrario suffered quite enough, we don't want history to repeat itself with you…'

A stream of tears trickled down Florinda's cheeks, which she licked when they reached the corners of her mouth. Esperanza took out the key and gave it to her.

'Take this, and forgive Elsa. She's only a girl, and there are lots of things she doesn't know.'

Florinda's face lit up.

'Thank you… I didn't realize Fernando and you…'

She stroked Esperanza's hand in gratitude, at which point Amadora came into the kitchen. She sensed there was some kind of complicit agreement between her daughter and her daughter-in-law, and was taken aback to find Florinda in the house at that hour. That said, she wasn't in the mood for asking questions, the answers to which she suspected she wouldn't like, so she limited herself to saying:

'Is that broth for Xuliano?'

Esperanza and Florinda nodded conspiratorially, sharing a silence, as if they were participating in a dark past. Amadora took the bowl and returned to her refuge of the last few weeks with resignation, aware that the clock was ticking down for Xuliano.

25

Dear Florinda,

Time passes, and here we are with the same urgent need to love one another, which becomes more and more difficult to bear. Not just the distance, but the fact you're married... I sometimes want to leave all this behind and present myself before that soulless wretch and demand what is my own, because before him you handed yourself to me unconditionally and, by the time I realized, I had already lost you... There is only one life, and ours is separated by something more than an ocean. It has been taken from us, my love. I'm tired of waiting. You ask for calm, and I am dying of impatience to cover your body with my kisses... But if you won't let me come and get you, then break your own chains, go ahead! I am waiting for you with open arms. You only have to say the word, and I will send you a ticket through our mutual friend, Isolinita... My love, don't put it off. Yours, in agony,

Rafael Xu...

Elsa had a pit of saliva stuck in her throat as a result of the emotion when she opened the gate to her house. Esperanza bumped into her in the corridor and saw she was upset.

'You look worried, Elsa. Didn't you manage to find the doctor?'

'I spoke to Mariola, and she said she would let him know. I'm going to my room, my head hurts a little.'

Esperanza was concerned by her daughter's downcast expression, but didn't think it right to insist. Elsa had always been a girl whose inner life was far too intense, as if inside her mind there was a bubbling pot on the verge of exploding. She watched her climb the stairs to the upper floor and wondered whether she should tell her that Florinda was in Sagrario's room and wasn't to be disturbed, but she kept quiet.

For her part, Elsa was convinced she had discovered another family secret – would there be any more? She rather thought there would. She started thinking many sorrows had been sown in that house and they were still parading around in the eyes of the women who had lived there before or inhabited it now. From Grandma Amadora, who wept for the war dead and blamed the living for still existing, and Sagrario, who had suffered her whole life for an innocent mistake, to Florinda, whose love had been taken away from her, leaving her dry, and her mother, Esperanza, who felt all of Grandpa Xuliano's resentment in her body for having married Fernando because of her background. Elsa's stomach shrank when she remembered she was the last woman in the Contreras Soler family and she was overwhelmed by the terrible thought, did she have sorrows in store? She shivered when she considered that her childhood had been terrible when it came to sensations and it would be impossible to melt the ice she carried inside.

When she reached the upstairs landing, she drove her thoughts away, because the contents of the bubbling pot had finally boiled over. She gazed at the door to Sagrario's room. She recalled the drawers full of brand-new shoes, which represented the loneliness of a woman who had been punished by her own. She felt tenderness. Then she recalled Florinda's sad expression and remembered Rafael's words. She felt envy. Would anyone ever love her with quite the same intensity? She said to herself that the only person in the house who deserved to have the key to that room was her aunt, and she regretted toying with her feelings by snatching it away from her. 'Break your own chains, go ahead!' she recollected.

But as Elsa was thinking, a few feet away, Florinda was not breaking chains – she was desperately ripping a mattress to shreds, searching for the only thing that gave her strength to endure the days and nights with their tedious hours, and she couldn't find it.

26

Elsa, entangled in the net of thoughts that assailed her on a daily basis, came to a halt on the landing in front of the door to the deceased Sagrario's room. She trembled like a leaf when she heard what sounded like a woman's sobbing coming from inside. She pressed her ear against the door, unable to believe what she was hearing, fearing it was just the product of her imagination that had been heightened by so many recent emotions. And yet the laments continued, and she had the impression there was rage or despair in them. Even that didn't make her entertain the possibility that it might be Sagrario's soul in there. She was still convinced there were no penitential souls doing the rounds of the house, since ghosts didn't exist. So who was crying in the bedroom? She didn't have the key to find out, and knocking at the door didn't seem appropriate. She rejected the idea of her mother, because she'd just spoken to her downstairs; Florinda as well, she never came around to the house in the morning, because Bieito left early for the factory and didn't like her going off on her own along the paths; apart from them, the only woman left was her grandmother. Elsa got to the conclusion that the sobs were coming from Amadora. She thought about continuing along the landing and not getting involved, but curiosity won out and she decided to give the door handle a discreet turn in order to check the moorings. She held her breath when she saw that the door gave way and pushed a little further until there was a gap she could peep through. She soon came across the tiny body of Florinda, who was sitting on the bed, crying. Elsa waited for a couple of seconds, enough to understand that Florinda, with or without Bieito's approval, had come to get her letters back and Esperanza had given her the key to the bedroom. And yet there was something that didn't fit. Why was she looking for them in the mattress? Perhaps that had been her usual hiding place and someone had gone to the effort of moving them? But what for? Elsa decided there was no point in prolonging Florinda's suffering and made up her mind to intervene. She opened the door and let herself be seen.

'Hello, Aunt. May I come in?'

Florinda, feeling defenceless and under the scrutiny of her niece's gaze, quickly dried her tears in an attempt to hide the fact she had been crying, but soon realized it would be tricky to justify the mess she had made of the mattress. She nodded and sank down where she was.

'Close the door.'

Elsa took a few steps forwards, removed the letter she had kept in her pocket and, coming alongside her, held out her hand and showed it to her:

'Is this what you were looking for?'

Florinda looked up and fixed her gaze on the sheet of paper. Before her thoughts could dictate a specific order, her hand had already gone out and snatched it from her. She got off the bed as if someone had pricked her bottom with a needle and unleashed a series of questions:

'How come you have it? Where are the others? Why did you move them?'

Elsa wanted to respond to the accusations, but Florinda's questions came flying out of her mouth. Her eyes were red from tears, and never had they seemed so similar to Sagrario's, so it was difficult for her to defend herself.

'I didn't move them,' she blurted out eventually. 'But I know where you can find the others.'

Florinda seized her niece's wrists with hands like claws. Her anxious expression, her panting breath and above all the pain reflected in her face inspired infinite compassion in Elsa.

'Don't suffer, Aunt. No one knows but me…'

27

Florinda found in Elsa's words and look the necessary confidence to calm down. She loosened her grip and let go of Elsa's wrists. Her niece responded with a placating smile and pulled her gently, like someone directing a child. Florinda let herself be led around the room while Elsa opened the drawers of the nightstands, the dressing table and wardrobe. Her face showed not a hint of surprise when she discovered their contents, so Elsa deduced she knew about Sagrario's passion for collecting shoes and possibly that they came from Fernando. She said nothing, waited to see what effect it would have on her to find her letters in the midsoles and forced her to play a game with her.

'Pick one, whichever you like,' she said, pointing to the open drawers.

Florinda held out her hand and lifted a random shoe into the air.

'Turn it around,' suggested Elsa.

Florinda went along with the suggestion and turned the shoe upside down.

'The sole is loose,' she remarked when she saw an opening on the side.

'Lift it a little and put your fingers inside,' Elsa invited her.

Florinda stared at her in amazement, but followed her instructions without saying a word. She soon felt her fingers coming into contact with something strange, which she identified as a piece of paper.

'Have you found it?' asked Elsa, knowing what the answer would be. 'Pull on it gently,' she advised.

Florinda didn't need any more explanations, since she knew at that precise moment exactly what she would find. When she had the piece of paper in her hands, she unfolded it with affection and, having verified its contents, kissed it again and again until she had ironed out all the wrinkles. The tears came back into her eyes, and she wiped them away with her sleeve before they should fall on the ink and spoil the contents of that treasure. She picked another shoe and repeated the operation, until she had half a dozen. The result was always the same, and she felt happier and happier at her discovery. She had time to reflect on the meaning of that find and, having reached the only possible conclusion, she spoke aloud, not caring whether Elsa heard her or perhaps thinking she deserved to:

'Sagrario felt she was fading away like a little bird, she knew she could die at any moment, and the poor thing wanted to protect me... She knew if this happened, the first person to enter the room would be my mother. She might move the bed or take off the sheets and discover the seam on the mattress, together with the letters... If she went and told my father, he might not like being reminded that his daughter was unhappy because of him... The poor woman hid them somewhere she thought it would never occur to Amadora to look... Perhaps she planned to tell me, but death came sooner than expected...'

Elsa felt the time she had longed for so much had finally arrived for another family secret to be revealed and saw that Florinda was preparing to empty herself completely.

'You have to understand, Elsa,' she went on as she released the letters from their confinement, 'your grandfather was no saint, despite the fact his mouth was always full of words such as "dignity" and "ideals"... He lost them both some time ago – first when he sentenced Sagrario to living in a niche, and then when he sold me to Bieito... Yes, don't look at me like that, my niece... You know the first story, but not the second, and, having got this far, I'm not sure it's worth talking about.'

Elsa knew if there was something it was worth talking about, it was this – to learn about the dark side to Grandpa Xuliano's personality – and she sensed Florinda was struggling with herself whether to keep her father's respectable image alive or to let go and rip off his mask.

28

Florinda sat at the foot of the bed and adopted an evocative tone to speak. Her eyes gazed at Sagrario's shoes, while her hands caressed the folds of paper that were piled up on her skirt.

'Who is Rafael Xunqueira, Aunt?' Elsa dared to ask. This was the only question Florinda needed to loosen the latch of her tongue, because as a torrent rushes down, sweeping along everything in its path, so did the flow of her words sound.

'Rafael is my love, dear Elsa, my true love… Bieito, on the other hand, my jailor… His accomplices, your grandfather and, to an extent, because she went along with it, your grandmother… When we were young, Rafael and I fell headlong in love. But there were no prospects here, so he decided to emigrate in search of a better future, with the promise that as soon as he was settled, I would go out to meet him; others had done the same, with success. His destination was Buenos Aires; mine was to wait for news of him. But that news was a long time coming, too long, I might add… At that time, your grandfather was involved in ill-considered business dealings. The consequences of his investments were terrible. The Contreras Soler family's heritage was at risk, and the only solvent person in the town who could grant him a loan was Bieito. That's right, Elsa, I mean Bieito, the one who would become my husband… I was the exchange. Bieito, who had set his eyes on me ever since I was a child, asked for my hand, and I had no choice… Rafael showed no signs of life, and your grandparents said the preservation of our patrimony rested with me. They sold me in return for the family home… I was bound for life to a dry, cold, man who sucked the youth right out of me. I died of sorrow, and every time my father passed in front of me, he lowered his head; Mother not so much, she's one of those who think you should endure everything for your family's sake, even if it means handing over your life… After half a year of being married, a childhood friend of mine, Isolinita Cruz, left for Argentina and, as luck would have it, she bumped into Rafael… She wrote to me and told me no sooner had the poor man arrived than he had succumbed to a dreadful fever that had kept him in bed for months, he had then been looked after by a charitable organization, had just found work and was in no position to offer me security. I cried my eyes out – I who had thought he'd forgotten all about me! With that letter, I came back to life, but I quickly realized there was no immediate solution – I was married, he was single, and the shadow of an accursed loan weighed over the family property. If I left Bieito, the creditors would flock to my father, and I didn't want to be the cause of my family's misery… Rafael learned about the situation from Isolinita and thought he would go mad… Months went by before he wrote to me. He did so very carefully by means of our friend. She was the one who appeared as the sender of the letters, but the words inside the envelope were his… We have been corresponding for years… Avelino the postman was our confidant, and Sagrario the keeper of the missives… We never lost hope of being together again one day, since Bieito, being much older than me, would eventually have to die, but our enthusiasm waned… Rafael was always much stronger than me… He never married, he's still waiting for me today, poor love…'

Florinda didn't continue her story, and Elsa felt the photo of Rafael Xunqueira burning the hand in her pocket. She decided she couldn't put off its return any longer and resolved to hand it over.

29

Bieito Nogueira never thought when he opened one of those letters that came from Argentina for Florinda he would feel such great satisfaction. He didn't find what he had been expecting – Rafael Xunqueira's words hidden behind Isolinita Cruz's name. And yet what the manuscript told him was revealing. He pondered for a moment and then decided not to go to the factory, but to wait for Florinda at home.

For her part, Florinda, having emptied herself in front of her niece, felt clean inside and secure in the knowledge that the letters were safe in the place Sagrario had found for them and it would be difficult for them to fall into a third party's hands.

'I think they should stay where they are. Sagrario's shadow will be their protector,' she said, getting off the bed and putting them back in the midsoles of the shoes. 'You know? Rafael hasn't written for some time, but if my intuition is correct, I think Avelino will have a letter for me today with good news.'

Florinda uttered these words with such a high degree of excitement her face became illuminated by a splendid light. Suddenly Elsa recalled she had seen Bieito coming out of the post office and mentioned it to her. She could never have imagined her words would cause such consternation in Florinda. Her face changed colour, and the letters she had yet to put back were scattered on the floor.

'Where did you say you had seen Bieito?'

'Coming out of the post office.'

Florinda could not explain to her niece why her intuition also told her Bieito had not gone to the post office to discuss his accounts with Avelino, but to lay hands on that letter. He must have noticed the postman's gesture as well! That was why he had been so understanding that morning.

'And now how am I going to show my face at home?' she said aloud.

Elsa couldn't understand her aunt's despair, but a single sentence of hers sufficed to make her aware of the situation.

'By this stage, Bieito knows Isolinita Cruz's letters are not from her, but from Rafael. What is going to happen now?'

Florinda was afraid to leave the room and walk back to her husband's estate. All the joy she had felt at Rafael's missive turned into anguish. Elsa wasn't sure whether she should say or do something, and it occurred to her to give her some encouragement by handing her the photo of Rafael Xunqueira. She took it out of her pocket and showed it to her:

'Have this.'

Florinda took the photo and gazed at it in surprise:

'Where did you get it?'

'From one of the shoes.'

'And what was a photo of your grandfather doing in Sagrario's shoes?'

Florinda's question collided with Elsa's face like a firework, it was so unexpected. The two of them exchanged a look of uncertainty. Florinda turned the photo around, read the dedication – 'Always yours, X.' – and found an explanation for many of the images of her childhood.

'The bastard!'

Elsa still couldn't understand. She tried to reflect calmly. She had found the photo of a man she thought was Sagrario's youthful love, with a dedication signed 'X.' She had then rejected this idea because she had come across the letters to Florinda, which were signed 'Rafael Xu...' She had quickly decided these two discoveries related to one and the same person – that is, Florinda – but now Florinda was telling her the image was not of Rafael Xunqueira, but of her grandfather… In which case, she concluded breathlessly, the 'X.' could only refer to 'Xuliano'. Why had Sagrario kept a photo of Xuliano in the midsole of a shoe? Florinda's curse gave her a clue, but she found it hard to believe… Her grandfather and Sagrario… Now it was Elsa who couldn't take any more. She ran out of the room and arrived just in time to throw up into the toilet bowl.

30

Florinda locked Sagrario's room and put away the key. She had to go home, even though she was afraid of the idea of confronting Bieito. She came across Amadora in the corridor. She was dressed in black, and Florinda noticed she had put the engagement ring Xuliano had given her when she was young on the index finger of her left hand, the very ring she had just seen in the ripped photograph Elsa had shown her... She felt a mixture of sorrow and shame. Did her mother know...?

'Are you leaving?' asked Amadora.

'I am,' she replied laconically, staring at the floor.

'Are you not going to pay your father a visit?' insisted her mother.

'I'm in a hurry,' she replied briefly and scuttled across the yard in the direction of the gate.

Esperanza watched her from the window and saw Amadora's defeated look. Both of them thought Florinda's expression had contained a mixture of incredulity and panic, but neither made any remark.

Florinda preferred to go straight home instead of stopping at the post office to confirm her suspicions. The discoveries of the last few moments weighed too heavily on her mind. She needed time to get used to them.

From the path, she spotted Bieito's car and wondered what he was doing at home at that hour. Her body trembled like a leaf. She advanced with tiny steps and found the door of the house ajar. She pushed it open and walked down the hall to the dining room, from where there was a cough. She came across Bieito smoking, sitting in his armchair with a serene expression, waiting for her. The whiteness of an envelope stood out on the table. On the floor, the worn suitcase with which Florinda had come to the estate after their marriage.

'Go back the way you came,' he spat at her calmly. 'There you have what is yours. An empty suitcase and a letter. Tell your father his debt with me is paid. I am handing you back just the way you came – without any luggage and in love with someone else who is not me.'

Florinda wasn't sure how to react. She had always thought Bieito would one day discover her long-distance relationship with Rafael Xunqueira and lose his mind, perhaps going so far as to kill her in defence of his honour. It had never occurred to her he would simply return her to her parents' home, sending her all alone along the pathways with a worn suitcase, having to endure the shame of neighbours' looks, which was her shame after all. And yet she felt relief. She went over to the table and lifted up the suitcase. It seemed full of air. Then the letter, which trembled in her hands and which she put in her pocket. Bieito blew out a cloud of smoke and said ironically:

'Enjoy the contents, it may be the last you receive. Isolinita has some news for you, which may be of great interest as regards your future.'

These words sounded like a threat, but suddenly she felt she had the strength to confront him:

'I'm not leaving as I came. You took away my life, does that seem little to you? But I'm still in time to…'

Bieito didn't let her finish and burst out laughing. Florinda turned her back on him and hurried along the path to her family's home. She wept and laughed. Laughed and wept. Esperanza saw her come into the yard without understanding a thing. Florinda entered the kitchen and sat on a stool. All she said was:

'I'm here to stay.'

And then she pulled the envelope out of her pocket.

Esperanza understood. Bieito had discovered her secret and didn't want to live with her in dishonour.

'Welcome,' she said, giving her a peck on the cheek.

Florinda took the letter out of the envelope and started to read. Tears sprang into her eyes. She shuddered. Esperanza thought she was crying for joy, but she was wrong.

'The bastard, that was why he was so happy!' she shouted in despair, remembering the feverish gleam in Bieito's eyes. Then she murmured in distress, 'Rafael, my love, Rafael…'

The letter fell out of her hands. Esperanza picked it up off the floor and read it. Isolinita Cruz informed her of the death of Rafael Xunqueira.

31

After vomiting, with the photograph of Xuliano in her hand, Elsa went downstairs with the intention of asking Amadora for an explanation. She knew she wasn't obliged to give her one, and yet she felt a rabid thirst in her throat to reveal the keys to the family secrets, sensing until everything was cleared up Sagrario's shadow would continue to wander about the house.

A certain premonition made her turn the door handle to her grandparents' room very slowly. The wooden leaf gave way silently, and the darkness drew her in. She took shelter there and hid in a corner. Amadora, with her back to her, was sitting in a chair, dressed in mourning, a hand of Xuliano's in her own, talking with shortness of breath and in a broken voice. As Florinda before her, Elsa noticed the ring that adorned her finger and no longer had any doubt that her grandmother was the woman missing in the photo, the one now murmuring:

'... I loved you so much I preferred to be blind than to shut the door of your exploits outside the house, but I never thought you'd dare try it on with Sagrario... Yes, you may think I didn't know, but I did... Those were bad times, and she looked after the children while I went in search of nourishment, why shouldn't she look after you as well...? What things am I saying, goodness me, the shame of it! I lost all sense of dignity...'

Elsa also felt ashamed for spying, but was incapable of leaving her refuge behind and listened carefully to the words of Amadora, who succumbed to a painful lament. Perhaps she wouldn't have to ask for an explanation and her words would suffice.

'… One morning, I came back earlier than usual and saw what I shouldn't have seen… The two of you in her bedroom… You were bestowing words in her ear I had never heard coming out of your mouth and kisses that had never left your lips to alight on mine… She gave them back to you with consuming passion and cried and, as she cried, she said "my love", and you replied "my love"… How I wept then! But I kept quiet. I didn't blame you. I always found an excuse to blame Sagrario for everything. I thought her apparent innocence was just a mask, a disguise to get you away from me… and then there were the children… I fell silent, awaiting my revenge. And it came… Those shoes that unleashed your wrath, despite your hidden love for her, those shoes that signified dishonour in your eyes, I gave those shoes to Sagrario, I took them off the dead woman, I handed them to my sister and made her promise to tell the version I wanted to hear, because I knew above the love you might have had for her there was the resentment you felt for others… She obeyed me like a little lamb, she knew I knew… And you reacted just as I had predicted. Your love turned to ice, you were repelled by the idea that she had once been your lover… I did nothing to stop her sentence. I thought her voluntary confinement would be my victory, but I was wrong… She suffered, you suffered, our children suffered… we all suffered. Ours was a life of darkness…'

Amadora noticed the coldness of Xuliano's hand in her own. She knew he had been dead long enough for everything that had left her mouth to have been swallowed up by the contaminated air of the bedroom. She loved him too much to make him suffer in his last breath.

Elsa wiped away the tears that were running down her cheeks and gave way to Dr Aneiros, who had come in time to certify her grandfather's death. She left the bedroom with the intention of opening the windows, of airing the bad omens and letting a fresh breeze into the house, but an image held her back. It was Florinda walking down the corridor in the same clothes Sagrario had worn before her. Her barefoot shadow made her blood run cold.

Read more titles in the series **GALICIAN WAVE**
published by Small Stations Press!

Francisco Castro, CALL ME SINBAD

Paulo's grandfather suffers from Alzheimer's. There are times
he forgets things, his head goes wobbly and his memories get
all mixed up. He even forgets who his son and daughter-in-
law are, but the one person he never forgets is his grandson, Paulo, even
though he calls him Sinbad the Sailor and they have adventures together
at sea (in the sitting room), fighting the filibusters. The other person he
always refers to is his brother, Bernardino, but Paulo's father tells Paulo that
Bernardino doesn't exist. Paulo's father is so busy at work he hardly has time
for the other members of his family and is always talking on the mobile, so
much so that his ear goes red. Even though he doesn't get home until eight in
the evening, he carries on dealing with work stuff on the phone. Grandpa has
these 'periods', moments when he deliberately knocks things over or won't
get out of bed or whacks the television on full-volume in the night. They drive
Paulo's mother crazy, but underneath she cares for him deeply. One day in
February, however, Paulo's family wake up to find that Grandpa isn't there
anymore, he's gone missing. It will fall to Paulo to have the adventure of his
life and find out where he's got to. This is the story of how a family copes with
the demands of an illness such as Alzheimer's, the changes that have to be
made. It is also a story of endeavour, of overcoming those filibusters – the
demons of daily life – that attack us at sea and finding strength where we least
expect it, in the contour lines of hope.

ISBN 978-954-384-109-7

Rosa Aneiros, BUTTERFLY WINGS

The Luzada, meaning 'shaft of light', is a café on the edge of the historical quarter in Santiago de Compostela, the capital of Galicia, a city that attracts pilgrims from all over the world. The café also has its share of cosmopolitan visitors and different languages, locals and migrants, who share the smoky atmosphere inside and the products of the coffee machine lovingly tended by Patricia, the tenant of the bar, who wishes she could receive love letters such as those Iqbal writes to his girlfriend in London. Everyone's fears and aspirations seem to find a shelter in this place, albeit some of them are laid openly on the table, while others remain hidden. There is Adolfo, who is separated from his children; Manuel, who sleeps 'in the cemetery', and his grandson, also called Manuel, who was adopted and is convinced his late mother has turned into a superhero; Filomena, the school cleaner who loves handing out sweets to the children and whose son is a UN peacekeeper; Paco and the taxi driver, who are constantly at each other's throats; Mohamed from Damascus in Syria, who runs a kebab restaurant and whose sister, Ghada, dreams of setting foot on the moon and licking it to see if it really tastes of goat's cheese; the tunic woman who turns up several times each day in the hope of receiving a phone call from her two nephews, economic migrants trying to reach Spain from Mt Gurugu; and then there is Aysel, the Kurdish girl who tells her boyfriend, Darai, the legend of Layla and Majnun, a story Lord Byron once described as 'the *Romeo and Juliet* of the East', and who is trying to find out information about her boyfriend, who has since disappeared. The owners of the bar, Lola and Eusebio, live upstairs; Eusebio has broken his hip and is confined to home. They all have different stories that, like threads in a garment or electricity from a patched-up generator, come together in one place and illumine our lives. *Butterfly Wings* is a patchwork quilt of shared humanity that emphasizes the kindness in people, understanding above conflict, in a world where local is global and our interdependence is clear to see.

ISBN 978-954-384-108-0

Iria Misa, SECRETS IN THE SUNSET

Mara's parents run the Sunset Hotel in Bico, a small town on the coast of Galicia. The Sunset Hotel is a family hotel, with old-world charm, the kind of place people come back to back year after year. Mara is almost eighteen and has taken the liberty of staying out all night and going to the disco with some friends. She has then hooked up with Tucho and brought him back to the hotel for a little intimacy, only her mother, who seems to have an inbuilt tracking device, finds out. The next day, Mara is unaware there has been an accident in front of the hotel, a hit-and-run. It just so happens that the victim of the accident is Tucho's previous (or not so previous) girlfriend. Mara for her sins is forced to do a stint in reception, where she checks in a hesitant, but not unattractive young man, Antón, who is staying with his mother and her husband. Mara and Antón become friends and investigate together the past of Mara's great-uncle, Paco, the previous owner of the hotel, who died some months earlier. It isn't only Mara's family that hides secrets, however, since Antón's family appears to harbour some secrets of its own. The summer holidays, which had looked like being a succession of boring revision classes, turn out to be much more eventful and illuminating than anyone could have imagined.

ISBN 978-954-384-106-6

Read more Galician literature in English published by Small Stations Press!

FICTION:

Anxo Angueira, LISTING SHIP
Xurxo Borrazás, VICIOUS
Carlos Casares, HIS EXCELLENCY
Ledicia Costas, AN ANIMAL CALLED MIST
Álvaro Cunqueiro, FOLKS FROM HERE AND THERE
Xabier P. DoCampo, THE BOOK OF IMAGINARY JOURNEYS
Xabier P. DoCampo, WHEN THERE'S A KNOCK ON THE DOOR AT NIGHT
Pedro Feijoo, WITHOUT MERCY
Miguel Anxo Fernández, A NICHE FOR MARILYN
Miguel Anxo Fernández, GREEDY FLAMES
Agustín Fernández Paz, NOTHING REALLY MATTERS IN LIFE MORE THAN LOVE
Paco Martín, THE THINGS OF RAMÓN LAMOTE
Teresa Moure, BLACK NIGHTSHADE
Miguel-Anxo Murado, ASH WEDNESDAY
Miguel-Anxo Murado, SOUNDCHECK: TALES FROM THE BALKAN CONFLICT
Xavier Queipo, KITE
Manuel Rivas, ONE MILLION COWS
Manuel Rivas, THE POTATO EATERS
Anxos Sumai, HARVEST MOON
Anxos Sumai, THAT'S HOW WHALES ARE BORN
Suso de Toro, POLAROID
Suso de Toro, TICK-TOCK
Xelís de Toro, FERAL RIVER

POETRY:

Rosalía de Castro, GALICIAN SONGS
Rosalía de Castro, NEW LEAVES
Xosé María Díaz Castro, HALOS
Celso Emilio Ferreiro, LONG NIGHT OF STONE
Pilar Pallarés, A LEOPARD AM I
Lois Pereiro, COLLECTED POEMS
Manuel Rivas, FROM UNKNOWN TO UNKNOWN
Martín Veiga, JEWELS IN THE MUD: SELECTED POEMS 1990-2020

For an up-to-date list of our publications, please visit
www.smallstations.com